Don't Forget **DEXTER!**

REALLY IMPORTANT!

DEXTER!

 LINDSAY WARD

two lions

For Jackson

Published by Two Lions, New York

www.apub.com

Amazon, the Amazon logo, and Two Lions are trademarks of Amazon.com, Inc., or its affiliates.

ISBN-13: 9781542047272
ISBN-10: 1542047277

The illustrations for this book were created using printmaking ink, colored pencil, and cut paper.

Book design by Abby Dening
Printed in China

First Edition
10 9 8 7 6 5 4 3 2 1

Is anyone there?

Oh, hi! I'm Dexter. Dexter T. Rexter.
Can you help me?

I'm looking for my best friend, Jack.
We came here together. For a checkup.
We were coloring and then I looked up and . . .

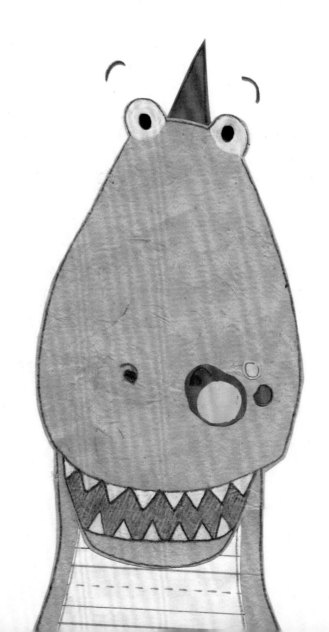

. . . Jack was gone.

It's been a
really long time.
Like forever.

Maybe you've seen him?

I know! I'll make you a picture.

How can you NOT remember him?!

He was just here!

I'm sorry. I didn't mean to shout.
Please don't go!

Hey! You think this guy saw him?

Excuse me. Hello? Mr. Fish?
Have you seen my best friend, Jack?

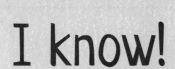

I know!
I'll ask this lady up there.
Bet she knows where Jack is.

Hello? Ms. Lady? Can you help me?

I know! I'll sing our song,
then Jack'll come back and find me.

DEXTER DINO, STOMP THROUGH THE SWAMP. DEXTER DINO, CHOMP, CHOMP, CHOMP!

He'll be here any second . . .

DEXTER DINO,
STOMP THROUGH
THE SWAMP.
DEXTER DINO,
CHOMP, CHOMP,
CHOMP!

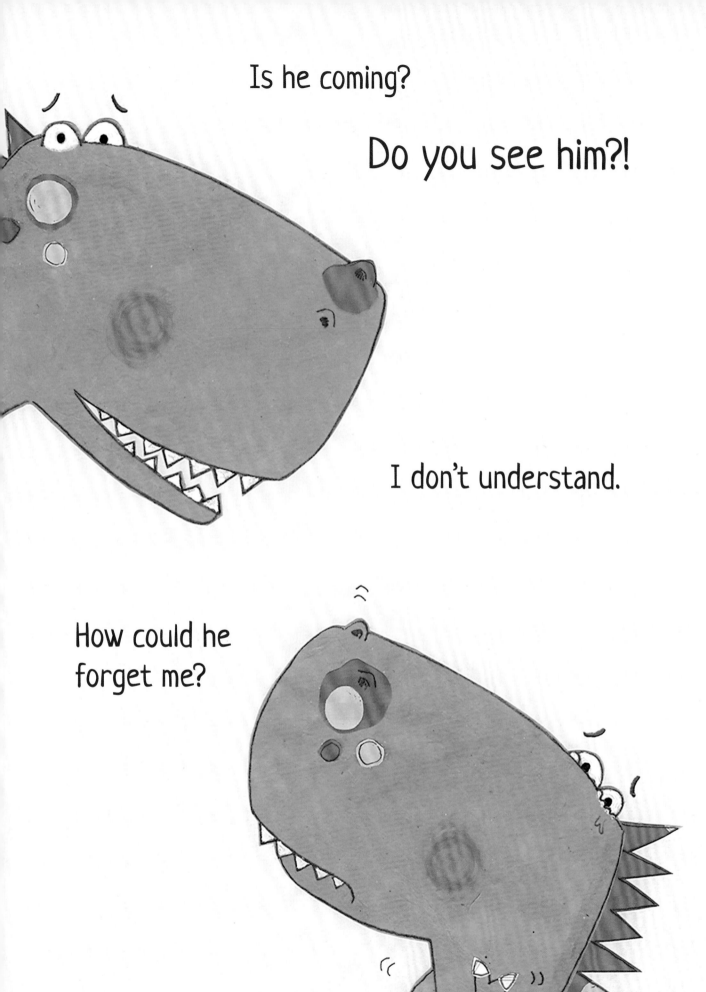

I sang our song!

Why isn't he coming back?

Oh no! What if he left me here

ON PURPOSE?

Nope. This isn't happening to me.

I'm Dexter T. Rexter.

The toughest, strongest, coolest dinosaur there has ever been.

EVER!

Right?

I mean, look at my tail.

See how
swishy
it is?

SWISH
SWISH
SMASH!

What do you mean,
maybe he likes something more?

More than me? Like another toy?

Oh no.

You don't think . . .

No! Not that, anything but that.

Wait, what did you say?
You think dinosaurs
ARE awesome?
Even better than trucks?

Really?

Me too.

I know!

MEDICAL SUPPLIES

BANDAGES

Wait right there.

Grrrrrr...

What if I never get out of here?

He's really never

ever

ever

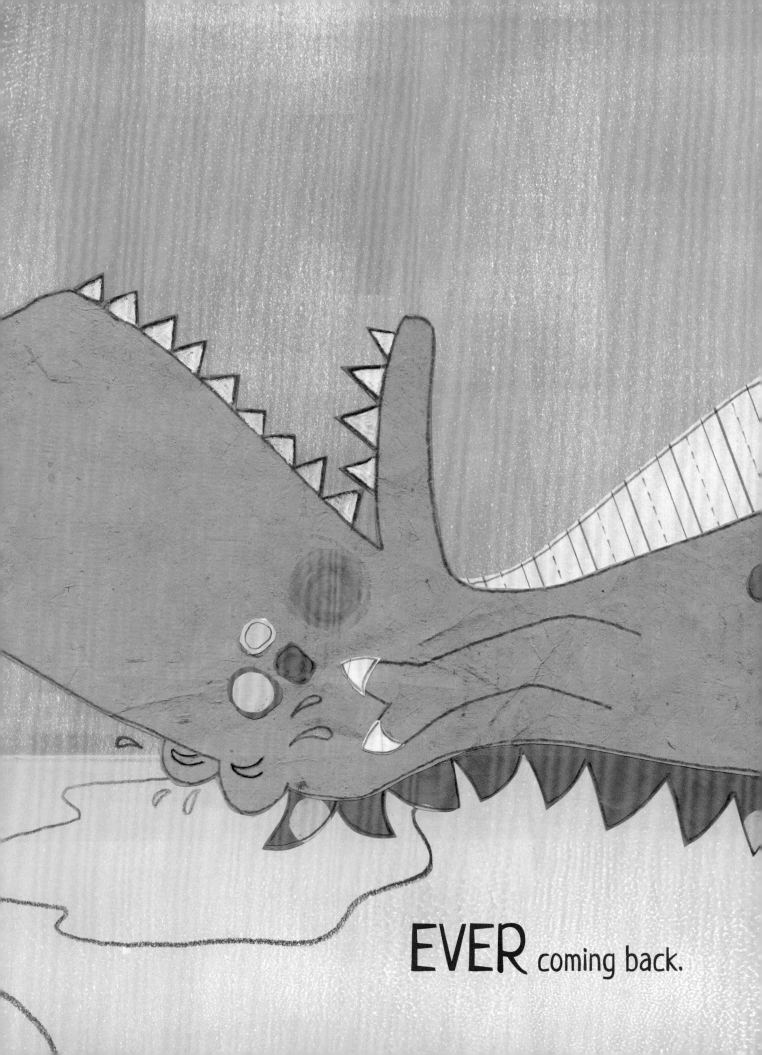

EVER coming back.

HE'S BACK!